williambee

Published by
PEACHTREE PUBLISHING COMPANY INC.
1700 Chattahoochee Avenue
Atlanta, Georgia 30318-2112
PeachtreeBooks.com

The illustrations were rendered digitally.

Printed and bound in December 2022 in China.
10 9 8 7 6 5 4 3 2 1
First Edition
ISBN: 978-1-68263-572-8

Cataloging-in-Publication Data is available from the Library of Congress.

williambee

Stanley's Park

PEACHTREE
ATLANTA

It's going to be another busy day
at Stanley's Park.

Stanley is watering the flowers in his greenhouse.

When they are just right, he
plants them in the flower beds.

They make quite a display!

Myrtle, Gabriel, and Peggy are doing their morning exercises.

Stanley has set the sprinklers to come on just after they have finished.

They had better hurry up!

Benjamin, Sophie, Little Woo, and Betty . . .

are doing their morning exercises too.

Stanley and Charlie are cutting and trimming the hedges.

It's lunchtime at Hattie's sandwich truck.
She has any flavor of sandwich . . .

as long as it's cheese.

The paddleboats on the lake are shaped like flamingos, swans . . .

and DRAGONS!

Back at the playground, Stanley and Charlie are doing their safety checks.

It's their most dangerous job . . . .

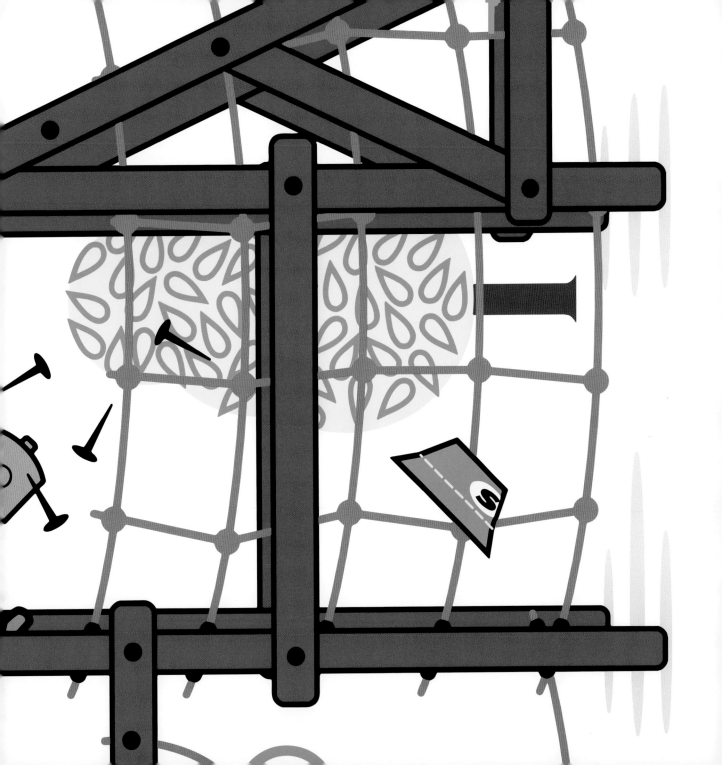

At last Stanley and Charlie get to sit down.
The sun is shining, the flowers are blooming . . .

and the band is playing.

Well! What a busy day!

Time for supper!
Time for a bath!

And time for bed!
Goodnight, Stanley!

Stanley

If you liked **Stanley's Park** then you'll
love these other books about Stanley:

Stanley the Builder
HC: $14.99 / 978-1-56145-801-1

Stanley's School
HC: $16.99 / 978-1-68263-602-2

Stanley's Garage
HC: $14.95 / 978-1-56145-804-2

Stanley's Train
HC: $16.99 / 978-1-68263-603-9

Stanley the Farmer
HC: $14.95 / 978-1-56145-803-5

Stanley's Fire Engine
HC: $14.99 / 978-1-68263-214-7

Stanley's Diner
HC: $14.99 / 978-1-56145-802-8

Stanley's Library
HC: $14.99 / 978-1-68263-313-7

Stanley the Mailman
HC: $14.95 / 978-1-56145-867-7

Stanley's Boat
HC: $16.99 / 978-1-68263-571-1

Stanley's Store
HC: $16.99 / 978-1-56145-613-8

williambee